THE
GEM
OF
FAITH

THE GEM OF FAITH

SEQUEL TO *THE RELIC OF POWER*

KEENON SOLOMON

Published by Mynd Matters Publishing
715 Peachtree Street NE
Suites 100 & 200
Atlanta, GA 30308
www.myndmatterspublishing.com

ISBN-13: 978-1-953307-82-8 (pbk)
ISBN-13: 978-1-953307-83-5 (hdcv)
e-ISBN: 978-1-953307-84-2

FIRST EDITION

To Amy Roberts,

The best grandmother anyone could wish for.

CHAPTER I

THE CAVE

Ever since locating *The Relic of Power* two years ago, Ronald and Susan have faced countless adventures together and been official partners. Their latest task included finding another elusive artifact, *The Gem of Faith*. Although they had no idea exactly what it could do, they knew the gem was extremely powerful.

For hours, they searched the northeast corner of the Amazon searching for the gem. After trekking without result, they finally came upon an enormous cave.

"You think this is it?" Susan asked as she approached with caution.

"According to my tracker, yes, this is it. Now let's get this over with," replied Ronald with relief.

"You seem to be in a rush," said Susan.

"Well, I have a movie to catch."

"And this movie is more important than your job?" Susan couldn't believe how unfocused Ronald seemed. It wasn't like him at all.

"I have to catch the matinee," Ronald said with a smirk.

As they slowly entered the cave, they were greeted by a terrible stench.

"Ugh! Was that you Susan?" Ronald joked.

"Ha. Ha. Very funny. I have a bad feeling about this so can we speed things up?"

The deeper they went into the cave, the colder and murkier it became. A mysterious mist surrounded them as Ronald eyed several small rodents and insects crawling from wall to wall. Startled, he jumped as something darted across his left shoe. He took a few seconds to calm his nerves again before continuing in the cave.

As they wandered, Ronald monitored the floor for booby traps and other unwanted surprises, while Susan surveyed the cave's walls. Suddenly, they came to a fork in the cave.

"Oh no, two identical tunnels. I've seen enough movies to know this isn't good," Ronald said.

"Can you see anything from here? Maybe we should split up. You can go through that one and I'll take this one," Susan replied.

"That's typically the option that doesn't end well but maybe it'll speed things up. Here, take this," said Ronald as he handed an extra light to Susan and walked over to the tunnel entrance on the right.

"Thanks and let's be optimistic," said Susan moving towards the tunnel to the left.

Even though they couldn't see much before they entered, walking through the tunnels was a different story. While Ronald's tunnel was full of bugs and rodents and had all kinds of plants growing from cracks in the ground and up the walls, Susan's tunnel overflowed with skeletons.

"Of course, I had to get the scary tunnel,"

Susan muttered to herself. She accidently stepped on a skull and a handful of weird insects surfaced.

As she continued walking through the tunnel, she became less worried about the ground and more about the insects climbing the walls.

CLICK!

Susan looked down to see her right foot on top of a well-hidden button. Before should had time to move, a net caught her and pulled her up to the roof of the tunnel. Then, the ground spread apart and small metal spikes rose from below. Susan looked down in terror as the net began to reverse direction and descend toward the spikes.

Susan had to think quickly, because if she didn't, she would not make it out of the cave alive. She thought for a second and soon figured out a solution to her problem. If she cut herself out of the net, she could grab the rope that was attached to the net and jump over the spikes. With no other option, she grabbed her knife and cut a hole through the net. She climbed out of it while tightly holding a piece of the net to keep from falling. She started to climb up the net and grabbed onto the rope. She looked down in fear knowing that if her plan failed, should wouldn't make it out of the cave alive.

The net kept lowering which meant Susan was getting closer and closer to the spikes. She had to hurry. She took a deep breath and jumped from the rope. She closed her eyes as she jumped because she really didn't want to see what was happening.

RIP!

Although Susan's landing was mostly successful, because she was alive, her right leg was cut on one of the spikes as she jumped. She winced and screamed in pain as she stood back up. She had to get out of there! As she limped through the tunnel, she reached down and could feel the blood seeping through the fabric of her pants.

While Susan dealt with her troubles, Ronald also struggled to get out of his tunnel alive. Unlike Susan, Ronald was cautious with every step, often spotting and easily avoiding the booby traps. But as he neared the end of the tunnel, a large rat ran across his path, startling him. All it took was a few seconds for his attention to shift before Ronald found himself hearing a loud and familiar, *CLICK!*

"Oh no!" Ronald said worried.

Immediately, a metal wall came down from the roof of the tunnel. It had spikes on the end of it and started to move towards the other end of the tunnel. The wall slid towards Ronald very rapidly and he ran as fast as he could towards the opposite end of the tunnel. He tried to avoid booby traps and make sure the wall didn't impale him. He was able to run a safe enough distance away to think of a plan to avoid it. He looked at the end of the tunnel and decided he would try to run towards it. As soon as he took a step, he accidentally activated another booby trap.

"You have got to be kidding me," Ronald mumbled with a groan.

A second metal wall came down from the roof

and started to move towards the other end of the cave. Now, Ronald was literally caught in the middle of the two spiked walls. What could he do? Then, an idea struck him. If he threw a grenade at the first wall, it could destroy it and he could run out of the tunnel. He wasn't sure it would work because it might collapse the entire cave but Ronald had very little choice. He had to do something as he was quickly running out of time. He grabbed a grenade from his vest and threw it at the wall. He covered his ears as the explosive rang out and destroyed the first wall. He could still hear the second wall coming towards him so he quickly jumped up and climbed over the large rocks and debris. He covered his mouth and nose as he tried to run towards the end of the tunnel without setting off another trap. He glanced backwards, seeing the second wall slowed down by the debris but still coming towards him. The trapped dust from the explosion make it harder to see but he knew the spiked wall was getting closer and closer.

Before it could impale him, Ronald made his way out of the tunnel and the wall abruptly stopped. He fell to the ground coughing and trying desperately to catch his breath.

"I almost died in there!" Susan yelled as she emerged from the tunnel and limped towards Ronald.

"Oh, you think you had it bad? You should see what I just went through in there," Ronald said through labored breaths.

"Well I have evidence. Look at my leg," Susan said, pointing at the large cut on her leg.

"Wow, that does look bad. Do you want me to wrap it up?" Ronald asked concerned it would become infected if it wasn't treated.

"No, let's just get this gem and get out of here. We'll take care of it later."

Ronald stood up and looked ahead.

"Do you see that?" He said to Susan.

She looked ahead and saw a bright, glowing green light. They both walked towards it, knowing it was what they were supposed to find. *The Gem of Faith* was a small yet bright enough to illuminate an entire room. Ronald pulled the gem from between a crevice in the cave's wall. He held it out as they both admired it.

"Wow! It's beautiful," said Susan.

"It sure is, now let's get outta here," Ronald said as he carefully wrapped the gem and placed it in his bag.

They only had one way to leave the cave and that was through the tunnel Susan had just survived. Their plan was to go as fast as possible while avoiding booby traps. Unfortunately, roughly ten feet in, Susan unknowingly stepped on a silent trap. Because there was no sound, Ronald and Susan continued running through the tunnel feeling closer and closer to the reality of life on the other side. All of a sudden, darts started shooting from the walls. One hit Ronald on the left arm as another pierced Susan's upper right leg. They tried their best to maneuver around the darts even at a slower pace but they couldn't avoid being hit. The darts were laced with poison, and if they were hit by too many, they would either pass out or die. Ronald was able to avoid the darts better than Susan, who became overwhelmed. As Susan's pace slowed more and more, too many darts hit her and she fell to the ground, passed out. Ronald turned around and saw Susan on the ground. He immediately ran back and picked her up, using his body to shield her from more darts. He ran full speed toward the end of the tunnel avoiding more hits. As soon as Ronald reached the outside of the cave, he placed Susan on the ground and searched through his first-aid kit to find an anti-venom. Once found, he put it in a syringe and quickly injected Susan.

"Please work," Ronald whispered to himself as the last drops entered Susan's bloodstream.

As he waited for Susan's anti-venom to kick in, Ronald removed the darts from his body. Once all of the darts were removed, he felt delirious. He knew it was the poison in his system so he quickly searched for another dose of anti-venom in his bag. He became more and more delirious, but then remembered the other vile was in Susan's bag, not his. Ronald clumsily opened Susan's bag to search for it, but before he could find it, he passed out.

Susan blinked multiple times as her eyes acclimated to her surroundings. She looked over to see Ronald on the ground passed and figured it was due to the poisonous darts. She didn't know how long he had been out so she quickly checked his pulse to make sure he was still alive. Fortunately, she felt a pulse and gave him the anti-venom. After a few minutes, Ronald woke up.

"Are you okay?" Susan asked him as they both struggled to stand.

"Yeah, I'm fine," Ronald said. "Do we still have the gem?"

Susan searched through her bag but it wasn't there.

"I don't have it," said Susan worried.

"Oh wait, I have it right here," Ronald said smiling.

"Great, now let's get out of here."

They walked to the meet-up point for their helicopter and headed home, with *The Gem of Faith* safe and intact.

CHAPTER 2

SECURING THE GEM

After a long helicopter ride, Ronald and Susan made it back to the museum and were excited to be safely back on land. Susan looked out of the window to see Martin standing near the helipad.

"How was the mission?" Martin asked as they walked towards him.

"Well, we almost died multiple times, so I would say…average," Ronald said with a sly grin.

"Great, can I see the gem?"

Ronald pulled the gem out of his bag and handed it to Martin.

"Wow! It is bright!" Martin said, shocked by the brightness of the gem.

He gave the gem back to Ronald and led them to the confidential artifact collection room where the gem would be stored, similar to the Relic of Power.

They walked through the museum which was full of tourists and employees.

"Why are we taking the gem here instead of putting it on display?" asked Susan as they walked past the display area.

"Even I don't truly know or understand the gem's power yet and until I do, it needs to be kept somewhere safe. Melody suggested here and I agreed," Martin answered.

He walked them to the edge of the museum and entered a four-digit pin to unlock a double-layered, steel door. As they crossed the threshold, Ronald handed Martin the gem and he placed it in a metal vault right next to the Relic of Power.

"So, can we go home now?" Ronald asked as they left the secret room.

"Not yet. I have a few things I still need you two to do in the museum," Martin said. "But first, clean yourselves up. You two smell terrible."

Martin was half-joking, half-serious.

After Ronald and Susan freshened up and changed clothes, they returned to their jobs at the museum. Ronald led tours and bragged about the artifacts he and Susan had found while Susan taught tourists and kids about the history of artifacts in the museum. It was an average day and all seemed to be going well until a suspicious black SUV parked right next to the stairs of the museum. The SUV appeared heavily armored and had no decals. After several minutes without anyone exiting the vehicle, the two security guards took notice and went over to question the driver.

"Hey, you can't park here!" one of the security guards said loudly as he inched closer to the car. The other stood back a few feet hoping the announcement would send the driver on their way.

As the guard got closer to the car, he noticed that all the people in the car were stone-faced and heavily armored. The driver opened the door and stepped out of the car. He slowly walked towards the approaching security guard. The guard backed away from the man because he was both scared and confused. The man quickened his step and ran up to the guard. He grabbed him and in an instant, snapped his neck. Before the other guard could react, the armored man, shot him in the chest. After both guards were down, four muscular and heavily armored men exited the cars, each carrying a weapon. Without a word spoken, they all walked towards the museum.

Once they got to the door, the men kicked it open and started to shoot up towards the ceiling of the museum. Security guards quickly came towards them, trying to fight them off, but they were no match as the five men were able to shoot them before they could do anything. Hiding under a desk, the receptionist sounded the museum's alarm to let everyone know they had to evacuate the building.

CHAPTER 3

AMBUSH

A larms blared all across the museum. Tourists started to flee and first responders rushed to the scene. No one quite knew why the men were attacking the museum so they didn't know what to protect. At the time of the attack, Ronald was giving a tour. When he heard the commotion, he lead his group to the back of the museum where they would be safe. They'd already walked through most of the museum but to get to the end, near the exit, they had to go through a dimly lit hallway. At the end of the hallway, they saw the silhouette of a man. The tourists were confused and scared and started to panic.

"Alright, alright everyone. I need all of you to stay behind me," Ronald said, trying to calm them down.

The group stood behind Ronald as he pulled out his pistol.

"Who are you?" Ronald yelled at the man.

The man didn't respond but Ronald noticed that he was loading a gun so Ronald shot a few rounds at him. The man ran from the bullets and hid behind a large metal crate.

"Go! Get out of here!" Ronald urged the tourists.

They ran out of the hallway as Ronald started to approach the man. He was terrified but he knew he had to try and fight. As Ronald approached, bullets started to fly towards him. Ronald was able to dodge some of the bullets but one hit him in the arm. Before the man could finish Ronald off, he was shot in the back by Martin.

"Ronald! Are you okay?" Martin yelled.

"Well, I was just shot in the arm, so not really," Ronald said sarcastically.

Martin ran over to Ronald and looked at his wound.

"It's just a flesh wound so you'll be okay."

Martin applied pressure on the wound with his handkerchief to stop the bleeding. As he tended to Ronald's wound, he noticed the tourists scrambling around, lost and confused.

"Hey everyone! Come this way! There's an exit over here!" Martin whispered loudly to them. Some of them heard him and ran towards the exit. Once the rest of the tourists realized what was happening, they ran towards the exit too.

While all of this was happening with Ronald, there were still multiple henchmen all across the museum. Multiple police officers were in the museum and they were searching all over for the men. The officers split up to cover more ground and two officers found one of the men. As soon as the henchman laid eyes on the officers, he shot towards them and they returned the fire. They had a series of back and forth until the henchman took them both down and continued walking through the museum.

As the other three officers went through the museum looking for the remaining men, they came across one of them and immediately fired their weapons. The man fired as well and was able to take down one of the officers, but the other two officers killed him. They congratulated their take down of the man but their celebration was premature as another henchman snuck up on them and shot them without hesitation.

Before the museum was ambushed, Susan was giving a history lesson to a group of children and tourists. When the alarms went off and gunshots rang out, neither Susan nor her class knew what to do and instead, they panicked. After a few minutes, Susan eventually snapped herself out of it and took control.

"Quiet down everyone! Okay, let's calm down," she said to the class repeatedly as she tried to get their attention.

After a bit, they looked at her, their faces all wide-eyed and scared.

"We are all going to stay here because we'll be safer in here, okay," Susan said.

"How will we be safe here?" One of the tourists asked.

Susan walked over to a secret door she had in her office that held her pistol. She grabbed it and loaded it with ammunition.

"Do you feel safe now?" Susan said as she cocked her gun.

Susan had her gun pointed at the door as she waited for whatever danger was on the other side to enter. After a few minutes, a foot forcefully kicked through the locked door. As soon as Susan saw the man, she shot him in his leg, incapacitating him. She quickly ran over to kick the weapon from near him and peeked her head through the door to see if any more henchmen were heading their way.

"It looks as if we're in the clear, guys," Susan said to the tourists.

Martin was still taking care of Ronald until he had a realization about what was happening.

"I know why they're here," Martin said.

"Why?" Ronald asked as he used his opposite hand to apply pressure on his wound.

"They're here for the Gem of Faith. I gotta stop them from getting it."

Before Ronald could respond, Martin sprinted to the other end of the museum to get to the secret artifact collection. When he got there, he saw a hole blasted through the door. He went in the room, hoping he wasn't too late. When he got inside, he saw one of the men holding a drone that held the gem. Martin shot at the man but the man ducked behind a shelf of artifacts along with drone. The man took out a grenade and threw it at Martin. When Martin saw the grenade, he kicked it and the grenade blew up in midair. The blast affected both of them and left them badly injured. The henchman was able to stand up and recover while Martin was still on the ground. Martin's face had been badly scarred and he was rolling on the floor in pain. The henchman walked up to Martin and stood over him. He then pulled out his gun and shot Martin until his clip was empty. Afterwards, the henchman put the gem in a small drone that had a designated location programmed in it. He walked out of the artifact collection room and into the hallway. He shot the nearest window and kicked out all of the glass before releasing the drone out of the window to its designated location. The alarm for the window alerted police officers of the henchman's location and they quickly came upon him and took him down.

CHAPTER 4

THE GAME PLAN

After the officers shot the last henchman, they went into the secret artifact collection where they saw Martin's body. Paramedics were rushed to the scene to resuscitate him but they were too late.

A week later, the museum was still closed and Ronald and Susan were at Martin's gravesite. They stood in silence staring at the pile of dirt Martin was buried under. They both shed tears as he was more than a boss to them, he was a true friend.

"We have to finish the mission, for him," Ronald said to Susan.

"How Ronald? The museum is closed and we have no clue where the gem is."

"The museum being closed doesn't matter, and we'll be able to find the gem. We have to finish this mission Susan, for Martin."

"How are we going to find the gem if we don't have the equipment we need? I mean, we don't even know who we're looking for. We have no clue who those guys were."

Ronald took a second to think about Susan's question and her comments. He didn't know how they would find the gem, but he knew they had to figure it out.

"We could ask Melody for help. I'm sure she can find out who those guys were," Ronald said

Something in his voice let Susan know he wasn't taking no for an answer. Susan was extremely reluctant to go on this mission because if those guys could kill Martin, they could kill them too. However, she knew she couldn't let the gem go with the bad guys and she could tell this mission meant a lot to Ronald, so she agreed to do it.

"I'm going to help you," Susan said. "You're right, we have to do this for Martin."

Once Ronald heard this, he became joyful,

something he hadn't been for the past week.

Ronald smiled at Susan and said, "We should get going. Call Melody and tell her she's about to have company."

*   *   *   *   *

Later that day, Ronald and Susan met up at Melody's house which was in the middle of nowhere. Her three-story brick house was far from any neighbors and was accessible by car via a lone dirt road which led to her driveway. The house was surrounded by a very large yard on either side and in the back. A ways out from the massive backyard was nothing but trees and forest.

"I'm so sorry for your loss," Melody said to them as they stood in the entrance of her home. "He was a good man. It's horrible to know what happened to him."

"You're right," replied Ronald. "And I want to avenge him so Susan and I came to you for help.

"You might just be in luck because while I was waiting for you guys, I found a possible location for the gem. Come in, I'll show you where."

Ronald and Susan followed Melody deeper into the house where they saw a map on her giant computer.

"The Gem of Faith is most likely here, off the coast of Guam. I believe it's with a group called The Hostiles. They are infamous for trying to steal artifacts from us. We don't know what their motivations are or who their leader is but we know they intend to do harm with the artifacts they steal. Every other time they've tried to steal from us they failed but this time it seemed to work," Melody explained.

Ronald and Susan took a moment to soak in all of the information. After a couple of seconds of silence Ronald said, "Now that we know where the gem is, we should go get it back."

"Unfortunately, it's not going to be that easy," Melody said. "We've sent two explorers before to take out The Hostiles and they didn't make it back. If we're going to get this gem, we need more than just you two."

"Are you saying we need a team?" Susan asked.

"Yeah, that's exactly what I'm saying," Melody replied.

"Well, who's gonna be our teammates?" Ronald asked.

"I know just the people," Melody said.

Melody proceeded to open up multiple files on her large computer, and soon four faces appeared on screen.

"These will be your new teammates," Melody said, pointing at the screen.

"The first one is an explorer from South Africa named Ashanti Bombwey. She's been working with us for nine years and has had multiple encounters with the Hostiles. She's an expert tactician and can hold her own in any fight. Trust me, she'll be a great ally."

The next explorer is Akira Saki. She is much

like Susan as she only started last year bu—"

"Wait a second. We're gonna have another rookie?" Ronald interrupted.

"What's so wrong with a rookie?" Susan said quite curiously.

"You know they mess up everything and you have to teach them so much," Ronald said sarcastically.

"Well, you're not going to have to teach her much because she is a very skilled fighter and quite resourceful. She is also gifted with technology and can hack into nearly anything," Melody said.

"These next two will also be joining you on this mission. The first is Juan Martinez. He's our explorer stationed in Guam and has had the most encounters with the Hostiles. He's worked with us for nine years and is an expert marksman and fighter. He can shoot nearly anything with pinpoint accuracy. The final member is Robert and he's stationed here in America."

"Really? Isn't Robert just a nurse?" Ronald

asked.

"Yes, and don't you think having a trained medic on the field would be helpful? Plus, he's not too bad of a fighter. He's also had several encounters with the Hostiles. I called all of these explorers up and we'll meet here in five days at noon. Understand?"

"Aye, aye, captain," Ronald said sarcastically.

"Don't sass me Ronald," Melody said.

"Anyway, you guys better be ready for this mission."

"Oh, don't worry. I was born ready," Ronald said.

Ronald and Susan said their goodbyes and went home to prepare for what might be the most dangerous mission of their lives.

CHAPTER 5

ASSEMBLING A TEAM

Five days had passed since Ronald and Susan showed up Melody's house to discuss the game plan and today was the day Ronald and Susan were set to meet the team. As Ronald and Susan walked up to Melody's door, they discussed their anticipations for their new team.

"You know Susan, I'm not feeling so hot about this team situation. I mean, I'm just warming up to working with you," said Ronald.

"Ronald, there's nothing to worry about. I'm sure this team will be just fine."

"I sure hope so."

They knocked on the door and waited. Although Susan was somewhat excited at the thought of meeting the other explorers, Ronald didn't try to hide his lack of enthusiasm. Melody opened the door and there they were, all four of Ronald and Susan's new teammates.

"Ronald, Susan, meet your team," Melody said pointing towards Ashanti, Robert, Juan, and Akira.

They were all in their explorer gear and each had a bag that housed their equipment. Juan's attire was extremely rugged, and his suit had several rips and tears. Ashanti also had lots of rips and tears but not as many as Juan. Akira's suit looked brand new except for one hole and her face read as if she'd never been on a mission in her life. Robert also wore the same bland khaki suits everyone else was wearing. Ronald's and Susan's suits were also very torn and beaten and looked much like Juan's.

After Melody introduced Ronald and Susan to their team, they all greeted each other. Susan tried to get a connection with everyone while Ronald avoided his teammates as he still wasn't comfortable working with a team. Akira and Susan immediately connected as Susan admired Akira's intelligence and Akira admired Susan's enthusiasm for the new team.

"What's up with your partner over there?" Akira asked as she noticed Ronald standing off to the side of the room.

"I don't know. He's never been that good at working with other people. I mean it took him forever to be willing to work with me."

"I can't imagine why he wouldn't want to work with you. I'm sure you make a great partner," Akira said.

"I appreciate that. Yeah, he can be pretty stubborn but he'll warm up to you. At least I hope he will," said Susan with cautious optimism.

Robert, Ashanti, and Juan warmed up to each other relatively quickly as they discussed their past missions. After a few minutes, Melody interrupted and asked for everyone's attention. It was time to discuss the details of the current mission.

"Since you guys have all met and had a chance to get to know each other, let's discuss business,"

Melody said as she pulled up a digital map of the Bering Sea.

"The Hostile's main operation is on this ship in the Bering Sea. The Gem of Faith may or may not be here, but if we infiltrate here, we can find out. Keep in mind, this ship will be heavily guarded either way."

"I'm not worried. We are some of the most experienced explorers in the land, right? This will be a breeze," said Juan.

"I hope you're right because I'm not willing to die for anyone's mistakes," said Ronald with a bit more than necessary assertiveness in his voice.

"Well if you're not willing to die on a mission, you shouldn't be an explorer," said Ashanti as she challenged Ronald's response.

"I'm willing to die for the gem, but not for you all." Ronald replied quickly and without remorse.

"Wow, those are some really strong ethics," Akira said sarcastically.

"I'm just saying we have no room for mistakes

on this mission. God knows what The Hostiles are doing with the gem."

"I do have a valid concern. If the Gem of Faith isn't on the ship, how will we find it?" asked Susan.

"We will hack into their computer files and find out where the gem is that way. I'm sure they have the location listed somewhere in their database," replied Akira with confidence.

"Now that I've briefed you on the mission, my job here is done," said Melody. "Discuss and plan amongst yourselves then you should be on your way. We have no time to waste."

Melody left the mission to Ronald, Susan, Juan, Akira, Ashanti, and Robert. And when she left, Ronald started to take control.

"Okay, as the leader of the group, I think we should—" Ronald said before being cut off by Ashanti.

"Who said you were the leader?" asked Ashanti.

"I mean, I did kind of start this whole

operation so I just assumed I'm the team leader," replied Ronald in a matter-of-fact tone.

"Okay, fearless leader, how are we going to infiltrate their ship?" asked Akira.

"The only way to effectively infiltrate their ship is for them not to notice us," said Ronald.

"Well that's obvious. I mean, I could've figured that out without you telling me," said Juan with a smirk.

"You didn't let me finish. I say we drop in from above and stealthily navigate through it," said Ronald.

"Does that mean skydiving because I really don't want to go skydiving?" This time it was Robert that spoke up.

"Yes, and isn't that exciting?" Ronald asked enthusiastically.

"I'm just a medic who can only somewhat use a gun. I still don't know why Melody brought me in for this mission," said Robert.

"Neither do I," Ronald retorted.

"Ronald," Susan said with a look that told him to focus.

"Okay, once we get on board, we have to be unnoticeable and we have to stick together," Ronald said to the group.

"Do we have the floorplan of the ship?" asked Ashanti.

"No, unfortunately we don't have a map of the ship," Melody said, injecting herself back into the conversation.

"So we're gonna have to wing it," said Juan.

"Well if we wing, it we'll have no idea of what's coming to us or what to expect." Robert's concern was palpable.

"Yep, so we're gonna have to trust our gut and try our best not to get caught," Ronald responded with confidence.

"We're not superheroes you know." Susan looked at Ronald who seemed all too ready to jump into a new fight.

"But we can fight like we are and that's gonna

be the only way we get this gem. Now let's get ready. We have a big day ahead of us," Ronald said as he turned and headed towards his equipment.

Two identical cars pulled up outside and Melody went out to meet them. The team grabbed their respective equipment and went outside to join Melody.

"They'll take you to a nearby hangar where the plane is waiting for you. On the plane are all the weapons you need. If something happens and you need more, go to this location and type in this code when you get there," Melody said handing Akira a tablet that had a location and a four-digit code which was 8416. Melody quickly said her goodbyes and watched the team drive away.

Once settled on the plane, they all prepared for what would likely be their most dangerous mission yet.

CHAPTER 6

TEAM PREP

The new team was embarking on their very first mission. The state-of-the-art plane had six separate compartments for each of them to rest privately as well as a main seating for the entire group. For the first few hours, the team kept to themselves and had very minimal interaction but after a while, Ronald called a team meeting.

"Now that we've had a bit of time to ourselves, we should talk strategy for when we actually get on the ship."

"Before we start, I just have one question. Are we going on the ship with the assumption that The Gem of Faith is there?" asked Akira.

"That is a good question," Ronald said as he thought about it.

"Maybe we should split up," suggested

Ashanti.

"Are you sure that's a good idea? I mean, doesn't strength come in numbers?" asked Robert knowing his chances were better with a skilled fighter or two standing beside him.

"That's true but we don't know where the gem is so half of us should search the ship for the gem and the other half should focus on hacking the files to see if the location of the gem is listed somewhere," replied Ashanti.

"She's right. I was thinking the exact same thing but she beat me at saying it." Ronald felt the need to save face as the group's de facto leader.

"How are we going to split up?" asked Susan.

"Akira, Susan, and I should hack into the computer and find out where the gem is while Juan, Robert, and Ashanti should look around the ship and see if it's there," answered Ronald with authority.

"Stealthily, I assume," said Robert sarcastically.

"Of course, we don't need anybody dying on

this mission," responded Ronald.

"I mean, we're infiltrating a highly-guarded ship with dozens of armed men. It's a high chance of death," said Robert while rubbing his hands together.

"Well with that attitude, we're definitely not making it," Ronald mumbled as he shook his head and rolled his eyes.

"How can we not be noticed? The ship probably has security cameras all over," said Ashanti.

"On the deck of the ship they shouldn't but once we get inside, that will pose a problem," said Akira.

"Can you dismantle their cameras from the inside?" Juan asked Akira.

"I can break into nearly any software on the planet. I'm sure I can hack whatever security system they have," Akira said confidently.

"I hope you're right, because if this mission goes sideways, it's kind of gonna be your fault," said Ronald.

"Thanks. That in no way adds any pressure," Akira couldn't help but reply with an annoyed sarcasm.

"And Akira, how do you expect to get into their files and find the location of the gem?" Juan asked.

"Did you not hear me when I just said I can break into nearly any software on the planet?"

"When we get on the ship, are the three of you just going to ransack it until you find the gem?" Susan asked Ashanti, Juan, and Robert.

"Robert and Juan will provide cover while I search the ship for the gem," said Ashanti.

"But it's a big ship. Do you really think you can look through it all?" Robert asked.

"Don't worry, I'll make it quick." Ashanti said. "Just do your job."

"Alright, does everyone know their assignment?" asked Ronald.

The team nodded their heads in agreement.

"Great! Let's get ready."

While the others were discussing the mission and preparing their things, Susan went to Ronald with her concerns.

"Ronald," said Susan.

"Yeah?"

"I don't think we have everything figured out here. I mean, we have no idea what could be waiting on that ship. I just don't think this is a wise idea."

"Well Susan, we have to get this gem as soon as possible because these guys clearly know something about it that we don't."

"I know that but something just feels off about this mission. If it were up to me, I think we should wait for another chance to get the gem."

"Susan, it's too late to turn around now so we just have to do the best we can." Susan's concerns weren't lost on Ronald but he didn't see another way forward given the situation.

"We're approaching the landing zone," the pilot said over the intercom, interrupting Ronald and Susan's conversation.

Everyone put on their parachutes and prepared for what was next. Someone came to unlatch the plane's door.

"Alright guys, make sure to deploy your parachutes on time and correctly or you'll be gone before the mission even begins. In terms of the mission itself, don't get yourself or someone else killed for being an idiot," and with that, Ronald jumped from the plane.

"Wow, how inspiring," Juan said cynically as he walked up to the doorway and jumped next.

Ashanti jumped next followed by Akira and Robert. Susan was extremely reluctant to jump out of the plane as she still wasn't convinced about the timing of the mission. She decided not to jump and stepped back from the door. Then an image of Martin came to mind and she knew she had to avenge his death. She walked up to the doorway and without hesitation, she jumped.

They fell from about 10,000 feet in the air and halfway down, one by one, they released their parachutes. Most of the team was tense as they left the plane but their nerves calmed as soon as their parachute deployed and they landed safely.

CHAPTER 7

BOAT RIDE

Once they were on board, Akira checked for security cameras. Just as she suspected, there were none on the deck of the ship. As the team walked around the deck stealthily, they spotted a group of five guards. The guards were dressed in all black and carried machine guns. All of them also had a mysterious bright green glow in their eyes. The guards stood lifelessly, as if they weren't human.

"What are they?" Susan whispered to Ronald.

"I don't know but we need to take them out…and quietly," Ronald whispered back.

Susan began attaching a silencer to her pistol and was preparing to shoot one of the men. Susan stopped as she realized the man had turned and was looking right at her. They locked eyes and she panicked and shot him. Unfortunately, she hadn't put her silencer on all the way and the gunshot alerted the other four guards.

"Oh no! Do you have any idea what you just did Susan? That gunshot may have just alerted the whole ship of our presence," Ashanti looked at Susan nervously as she spoke. They both bent down lower trying not to be spotted.

The other four guards looked at the dead body of their comrade. Their faces lacked any human expression. As they looked down, a flashbang grenade rolled towards them and detonated, temporarily blinded them. While they were blinded, Ashanti and Juan shot all four. This time, with their silencers on. When the guards died, the green glow in their eyes dimmed and their eyes returned back to normal. Juan and Ronald grabbed the bodies of the men and threw them overboard to hide the evidence.

"Let's go!" Ashanti whispered.

The Explorers ran through the ship taking out

guards and throwing them overboard along the way. After a few minutes of going around the deck of the ship, they found an entrance. Akira covertly approached the door noticing the security camera overhead. She pulled out her tablet and pressed several keys before disabling the camera.

"I thought you said there would be no cameras on this ship," Susan said to Akira.

"I said on the outside of the ship. I'm sure the inside of this ship is crawling with cameras."

After Akira disabled the camera, the team proceeded to go inside one by one.

Once inside the ship, they found out that everyone was on high-alert due to the gunshot. They team hid in a corridor and saw a few Hostiles heading outside to check the deck of the ship.

"They're going outside and it won't take long for them to notice the missing guards," Susan said.

"Well, all the more reason to hurry this up," said Juan.

"Alright, let's split up and do our jobs," Ronald

whispered quietly to the team. "Oh, and do me a favor…don't die."

As Ronald instructed, the team split up and went to fulfill their respective tasks. Ronald, Susan, and Akira ventured through the grimy and dark hallway of the ship looking for the main control room.

"How is there water leaking from the ceiling? We're on a boat," said Ronald as water dripped on him from above.

"Be quiet before someone hears us," responded Akira.

They continued down the dirty and cluttered hallway, as the lights flickered on and off. Ronald, Susan, and Akira watched their steps and kept checking different rooms to see if they were the control center. After they checked all the rooms on that hall, they turned the corner ready to check the other hall. Before they could take another step, they were spotted by four Hostiles with bright green eyes. Ronald, Susan, and Akira pulled out their pistols, and so did the four Hostiles. Gunshots rang out as both sides fired their weapons. The green eyes of the Hostiles impacted their vision and their target accuracy was that of a stormtrooper. Since The Hostiles' accuracy was terrible, the team was able win the shootout and take out the four Hostiles.

"Well I don't think we're doing this very stealthily anymore," said Akira.

While Ronald, Susan, and Akira continued their search for the control center, the rest of the crew searched the ship for the Gem of Faith. They looked through nearly half of the rooms and found nothing.

"This is one long ship. How many rooms are in here anyways," Juan stated.

Ashanti replied, "Enough to hide one of the most powerful artifacts on the planet."

They kept walking through the hall and found a room they hadn't searched yet. The team searched it and like all the other rooms before it, they found nothing.

"Alright this is getting ridiculous. All these rooms and none of them have the gem," Juan said frustrated.

"We still have about twenty rooms to go so let's get a move on it," Ashanti whispered.

They continued to look room by room. Suddenly, they walked into a room that was occupied with five Hostiles. The five men drew their weapons and fired at the Explorers. Just like the other Hostiles before them, the five men all had green eyes and horrible accuracy. The only light in the room were the flashlights Robert, Ashanti, and Juan were holding so they had the advantage. The gunfight with the Hostiles didn't last long as Ashanti shot two of the men and Robert and Juan shot the last two. When they finished, they searched the room and still found no gem.

While the rest of the crew searched the ship for the Gem of Faith, Ronald, Susan, and Akira had located the control room which housed the main computer. The massive room was dark and illuminated only by the bright blue screens of the computers. Four monitors covered one of the walls and when Akira saw them, a huge grin spread across her face.

"I assume this is it," said Ronald.

"Sure is," Akira said. "Now let's see if that gem is here or somewhere else."

Akira broke through the computer's firewall fairly quickly.

"That was quick." Ronald was genuinely impressed by Akira's skill.

"This type of stuff is my forte," said Akira.

"Can you see where the gem is?" asked Susan still recognizing they had limited time.

As Akira searched for any files pertaining to the gem, she found something very interesting. Susan noticed a change in her facial expression.

"What is it? What do you see?" asked Susan.

"They have plans to take it to Alaska but... give

me one minute. Okay, yeah. From what I'm seeing, the gem is still on this ship," said Akira.

"What are they planning?" asked Ronald.

"Something very big." The unexpected response came from behind them, towards the door.

The crew immediately drew their weapons as soon as they heard the unfamiliar voice. The man was short with black hair and was wearing a black athletic shirt with cargo pants. Behind him were six henchmen with bright green eyes, like the others.

"You all seem awfully defensive. Now Ronald, tell me what exactly do you want with this?" The man asked holding up the Gem of Faith.

"How do you know who I am?" Ronald asked with confusion in his voice.

"Everyone knows of the great Ronald Moore and his wonderful partner, Susan Kline. Although, I don't quite know who *this* is," he said pointing at Akira. "But it won't matter because you'll all be dead soon. Oh and the name's Tavin Braxt."

"I don't think so but I have another option. How about I get that gem and be on my way," said Ronald.

"Really? Because to me it looks like you're outgunned," said Tavin as he gestured towards his men.

"Nah, I brought back up," said Ronald.

A look of concern flashed across Tavin's face and then he heard gunshots from behind. One of his men went down and the other men turned around and returned fire at Juan, Ashanti, and Robert. They engaged in a violent shootout with the men but since The Hostiles were being attacked from the front and the back, they were quickly taken down. Tavin put the gem in his pocket and ran out through the glass wall to get away from the Explorers.

Ronald headed after Tavin, "Don't go after him, we need you to fight with us!" yelled Ashanti.

"He has the gem. I can't let him get away," he yelled back before running out through the same glass exit.

Ronald chased after Tavin focused on retrieving the gem. After the team finished off the Hostiles in the room, alarms blared all across the ship and dozens of Hostiles rushed down the halls to their location.

Ronald was still running after Tavin and when Tavin noticed, he shot back in Ronald's direction. Tavin shot very wildly and inaccurately and not a single bullet hit Ronald but it did slow him down since he had to duck for cover.

While Ronald chased Tavin, the rest of the team prepared for all of the Hostiles heading towards them.

"Be ready guys! Shoot anyone who comes this way," yelled Ashanti to the group.

The crew stood together in an outwardly facing circular formation and when Hostiles came into the room, all hell broke loose. Bullets flew everywhere and the Explorers were holding their own. Although the team was very aggressive in their attack, the soon were outnumbered by the Hostiles. They disbanded the circle and ducked for cover.

"How are we gonna get rid of them?" Juan shouted.

"I have a bomb in my bag but you guys need to hurry up and get out of here!" Akira shouted back.

Akira and Susan placed the bomb on the wall and Akira set a thirty second timer.

"Guys, let's get out of here!" Akira yelled.

The whole crew ran out of the control room in the nick of time before the bomb exploded. The bomb destroyed the control room and obliterated all the Hostiles in the room. It also destroyed the ship's computer.

"Wait. You're telling me you had that thing in your bag this whole time?" Juan said to Akira.

"Yep. I always have a back-up plan."

In the midst of the commotion, Ronald was still going after Tavin. When Ronald heard the explosion in the control center, he became worried for his teammates but couldn't dwell on it because he had to catch Tavin. After some more running, Ronald finally caught up to Tavin and tackled him from behind. Ronald got on top of him and started to deliver a flurry of punches to his face and body.

"It's over now, Tavin! Give me the gem!" said Ronald.

"I don't think so," said Tavin as he grabbed the Gem of Faith from his pocket and pointed it at Ronald's forehead.

A green beam shot from the gem and onto Ronald's forehead. Tavin started to stand up and as the beam from the gem moved Ronald off of him. Ronald's head was in extreme pain, and he couldn't move. He actually couldn't do anything except stand completely still, while Tavin got everything he wanted.

CHAPTER 8

ALTERING FAITH

After the Explorers blew up the control room they decided they needed to check on Ronald.

"Where is Ronald?" Susan asked.

"I saw him going after that Tavin guy," answered Juan.

"Let's go find him," said Susan.

The team all went down the same hall following the path Ronald and Tavin had taken.

Unbeknownst to them, Tavin was using the Gem of Faith on Ronald. Ronald stood completely still and in intense pain. He couldn't even scream as the Gem penetrated his skull and altered his brain. Suddenly, the beam disappeared and Ronald fell to the floor. His eyes shut and his body went cold, as if he'd died.

Tavin grinned as he saw Ronald on the ground because he knew he had just won. After a few seconds of Ronald being in a comatose state, his eyelids shot open and instead of his normal eye color, his eyes were now the same bright green as the Hostiles. He stood slowly with a blank expression and the pain he had felt on his head was now gone. He turned towards Tavin.

"Hello Ronald, you work for me now," said Tavin in a sinister tone.

"Yes," replied Ronald in an emotionless and robotic voice.

"I want you to kill your newly-found teammates. Then, you will come with me," Tavin said to Ronald who he now controlled.

While all of this was going on with Ronald and Tavin, the Explorers were searching the ship for any sign of Ronald or the gem. They decided to split up, hoping to cover more ground. As Susan went through a well-lit and spacious hallway, she saw the back-side of Ronald.

"Ronald!" Susan said excitedly.

She ran up to Ronald happy to see him but then he turned around. Susan immediately noticed his bright green eyes and expressionless face.

"Ronald?" Susan said as she backed up nervously.

Ronald pulled out his gun and pointed it at Susan's head. She grabbed Ronald's hand and held his gun down. Susan tried to wrestle the gun out of his hand but Ronald was stronger than her so he was able to keep the gun in his hand. Ronald once again pointed the gun at her face but instead of trying to wrestle the gun away from him, she just punched him in his jaw. This staggered Ronald long enough for Susan to land a few more blows. She was able to hit Ronald in the face two more times before he caught her punch. When he caught her punch he twisted her wrist and Susan fell to her knees while screaming in agony. Ronald hit her upside the head with his gun, knocking her to the ground. Susan thought this was about to the end as she laid defenseless on the ground while Ronald had a gun pointed at her. However, before Ronald could pull the trigger and kill Susan, bullets started flying from behind him. Ronald ran and ducked for cover and started to shoot back. The ones who were shooting at Ronald were Robert and Akira. At first they thought they were shooting at a regular Hostile, but when they saw Ronald's face, they were confused and they hesitated. When they hesitated, Ronald shot Akira in the arm.

"Akira!" Robert shouted.

He picked up Akira and ran for cover. Ronald continued shooting at them, but his green eyes derailed his accuracy. When Robert got to cover, he got out his first aid kit and applied pressure on Akira's arm.

"Am I going to be alright?" asked Akira.

"Yes, it's just a flesh wound. You'll be fine."

"Why is Ronald doing this?" Akira asked. "And why are his eyes green?"

"I don't know but we need to stop him," said

Robert.

Ronald walked towards Akira and Robert but before he could reach them, he was kicked in the back by Juan. This nearly knocked Ronald down but he was able to catch himself. His gun fell out of his hand. Juan pointed his gun at Ronald but Ronald kicked the gun out of his hand. They then got into a brutal hand to hand fight. Ronald and Juan were both very skilled fighters so a lot of their punches didn't connect as they were both skilled at defending themselves. Juan finally landed a punch to Ronald's gut and he then tried to get Ronald to the ground. Juan ran up and tried to tackle him, but Ronald was able to throw him off. Juan fell to the ground hard and he fell on his head. When Juan fell, Ashanti ran up and kicked Ronald in the chest.

Ronald's and Ashanti's fight styles were very different. Ashanti used acrobatics and flexibility in her fighting. Ronald, however, used his brute strength and boxing ability in fighting. Ashanti landed more blows than Ronald, but his blows left more of an impact than hers. Ashanti was repeatedly kicking and punching Ronald and it seemed as if she was winning until Ronald grabbed her leg mid-kick. Ronald threw her across the room, got on top of her, and started to wail on her. Punch after punch after punch to her face. Juan saw this and knew he had to do something. Juan's head was still in pain but he got up regardless and he grabbed a large metal pipe and ran up to Ronald. Before Ronald noticed, Juan hit him in the head with the pipe and knocked him unconscious.

"Are you okay?" Juan asked Ashanti.

"Yeah," said Ashanti pained by the assault. Her face was badly bruised.

Juan helped her to her feet.

"You need a doctor," he said.

"We don't have time. We need to hurry up and get off this ship," said Ashanti.

"We can't. We don't have the gem yet," Juan said.

"If we're going to get it, we need all of our

teammates. Let's go find them," said Ashanti.

Ashanti and Juan split up to gather the rest of the team. Ashanti ran to Susan who was sitting in the corner of the room still shaken from the fight that had just happened.

"Susan, are you all right?"

"What did that man do to Ronald?" Susan said ignoring Ashanti's question. "We have to get Ronald back and find out what this guy did to him."

"We have to get the gem first," said Ashanti.

"Did you not see what just happened? That man Tavin is controlling Ronald with something and we have to figure it out now." Susan was angry and confused, all at once.

"Susan, our mission is to get the gem. We'll worry about Ronald after we find it. Now let's hurry before more Hostiles come."

"Okay, but you have to promise me we'll come back for Ronald," said Susan.

"I promise, now let's get with the others."

While Ashanti got Susan, Juan went to help Robert and Akira.

"C'mon guys, get up," said Juan. Then he noticed Akira's gunshot wound and apologized.

"I'm going to be fine," said Akira reassuringly.

She stood up with the help of Juan and Robert and then they went to find Ashanti and Susan.

"Why were we just attacked by Ronald?" Robert asked furiously.

"I think that's what the rest of us are trying to figure out," said Susan.

"Where is he now?" asked Akira.

"Over there," said Ashanti as she pointed towards his unconscious body on the floor.

Juan looked over at Ronald's lifeless body.

"Let's grab him," he said.

"No, we have to get the gem first then we'll come back for him. Now let's go," said Ashanti as she grew more impatient.

The team moved back towards the long hallway but were suddenly interrupted by gunfire.

A large horde of Hostiles had found them and were on the attack. The Explorers ran through the hallway, dipping in and out of rooms and behind large crates, avoiding gunfire as best they could.

"Um…you wouldn't happen to have another one of those bombs would you?" Susan asked Akira.

"No, it was a one-off," Akira shrugged her shoulders as she answered.

"Turn the corner!" Ashanti yelled.

The team turned the corner and crouched behind anything they could find, waiting for the Hostiles to approach. Once the Hostiles turned the corner, they were met with gunfire. The Explorers aimed for the legs as they didn't want to slaughter them, but they were able to mow through them and continued towards the deck of the ship.

"Run! Our ride is here!" Akira yelled to the team as they continued towards the open deck of the ship.

At some point during the commotion, she had

dialed the code for their pickup. Even though they flew in undetected on a plane, a helicopter was their best chance of escape so it had been circling nearby. They ran towards the swinging ropes and grabbed on. Each climbed up as the helicopter flew away, leaving the ship and the remaining Hostiles in the far distance.

The helicopter took them to a secret hangar where their plane was fueled and ready to take them home. Although alive, the Explorers were still shaken from what they'd just experienced.

"Where's Ronald?" the pilot asked as they all settled into their seats.

"It's a long story," Juan said before collapsing into a chair and dozing off.

The pilot looked at Susan with utter confusion. She shrugged her shoulders and leaned back in her seat wondering what exactly they planned to do next.

CHAPTER 9

ALL THE POWER

Ronald blinked a few times trying to get his bearings. He felt like he was coming out of a haze of some sort. He started to move but realized he was sitting in a chair with his hands and feet handcuffed. On either side of him was a Hostile standing guard. Several Hostiles were also moving about in the distance with boxes and large tools.

Ronald would soon discover that he was at the Hostile's base site. Even though he was struck by the dull beige color of everything around him and the freezing temperature, both were the least of his concerns. He blinked again and tried to move his hand towards his head to remedy the throbbing pain but was reminded of the handcuffs. The last thing he remembered was a green beam shooting at his head.

"Hello Ronald," said Tavin as he walked up to him.

"What did you do to me?" Ronald said angrily.

"Oh, well I just used this little beauty right here," Tavin said, holding the Gem of Faith between his thumb and forefinger.

Ronald winced as he stared at the gem. His memories became clear and he remembered fighting Susan, Akira, Ashanti, Robert, and Juan.

"Why was I fighting my own team? I tried to kill them. I-I…tried to kill Susan," said Ronald, confused and terrified.

"That's because I used the Gem of Faith on you. You see, this small yet powerful gem has the power to alter your mind and whoever uses it on you has complete control on what you believe. I made you believe in my goals, therefore, you had no choice but to do my bidding, " Tavin explained.

"But why control me?"

"Because you're the best explorer there is and you would be a great asset to my cause.

Furthermore, I could tell you didn't believe in your little team of explorers."

"What does my belief in my team have to do with anything?"

"Belief has everything to do with it Ronald. You didn't *believe* your team would succeed so that means you didn't have much faith in them or yourself. When you don't believe in what you're fighting for, you can be easily influenced by the gem."

Ronald thought about what Tavin said and although he hated to admit it, Tavin was right. He really didn't have any trust in his team, except for Susan. Even though he knew his lack of faith was precisely what enabled Tavin to control him, he still didn't believe his team would be able to pull off the mission, especially since he wasn't with them.

"Why are you controlling people with the Gem? Is everyone here being controlled too?" Ronald asked, referring to the henchman all around him.

"The world needs structure, it needs order under one person. Right now, people run wild and what does that get you? War, crime, and chaos. If someone doesn't step in now, the world will tear itself apart."

"The world? How are you going to control the whole world?"

"Good question. It would be a daring task to control millions of people. I mean, it took me years to accumulate this small militia. That's why I'm going to use a satellite dish to spread the gem's power for millions of miles, putting millions of people under my thumb."

"If you do that, you'll take away people's free will. We'll be nothing more than mindless animals."

"But Ronald, that's what the world needs—the elimination of free will."

Ronald knew Tavin was too far gone and there was no reasoning with him. Ronald had seen tyrannical men before, but none like Tavin.

"You won't win, Tavin. The Explorers will stop you and this ridiculous plan of yours."

"How will they have time to fight me, when they're too busy fighting you?" Tavin said with the Gem of Faith now raised towards Ronald.

Tavin pointed the gem at Ronald's head and like before, a green beam of energy shot from the gem and onto Ronald's forehead. The beam's energy was painful at first, but faded away in a few seconds and Ronald's mind was overtaken by the gem yet again. When the energy beam stopped, Ronald slumped over, his eyes closed, and his body cold. Within a few seconds, Ronald popped right back up, opened his eyes, and they were bright green. Ronald was now under Tavin's control.

"It's good to have you back Ronald," said Tavin as he uncuffed Ronald.

"Thank you sir," Ronald said in monotonous, almost robotic voice.

"With your help, we will spread the Gem of

Faith's power all across the continent. Now go help build the satellite with your fellow soldiers," Tavin commanded.

Ronald obeyed and went over to help construct the massive satellite dish they were building.

The Hostile's base was situated near the mountaintop of Mount McKinley. Although Ronald followed the trail of the other Hostiles, he felt an energy pulling him to the satellite's location. He scaled the mountain to reach the satellite and while it was beyond freezing up there, Tavin had given him a coat and gloves to withstand the temperature. The other Hostiles didn't have the same luxury and had to construct the satellite in the cold with barely any protection. Hundreds of Hostiles worked on the mountaintop, all of them had bright green glowing eyes and were under control of Tavin and the Gem of Faith. Because Tavin controlled their focus, they were able to withstand the cold as the only thing on their minds was constructing the satellite. These men had complete faith in what Tavin believed and would do anything to accomplish his goals. Tavin was seen as a king amongst the mindless henchmen and he knew that soon, when his plan was complete, he would be seen as a king in the rest of the world, too.

CHAPTER 10

REGROUP

On their plane ride home, the Explorers were in a combination of shock and disbelief. They spent the majority of the ride in silence, reflecting on everything that happened and their unexpected loss of a crew member.

Susan was the most difficult time as she couldn't stop thinking of what may have happened to one of her best friends, a person who was like a father-figure to her. She sat in the rear of the plane with her back facing everyone. Her thoughts were consumed with what unknown torture was happening to Ronald. She grew increasingly upset with Ashanti for not going back to get Ronald.

After a couple of hours of the team sulking in their defeat, they landed at a nearby base of operations in Yukon, Canada. The crew unloaded the plane and went into a nearby building. It was a drab gray, mid-sized building in a remote part of Yukon, which didn't have another town for miles.

"Signal me if you need me, I'll be in the plane," said the pilot as the team walked towards an entrance point on the base.

The team went through the retinal scan at the entrance and walked down a short hallway. After a few feet, the lights flickered above and then came all the way on. They pushed open the next set of doors and were surprised to be surrounded by nothing but weapons and artillery. They soon realized that they were at a state-of-the-art weapon's base. Before them were shelves and shelves of guns, grenades, drones—you name it. The Explorers looked around, more hopeful than they'd been just minutes before. They walked across the hard metal floor and gathered at a rectangular black table in the center of the room. It was time to decide their next move.

Ashanti looked at Akira. "Akira, you said they

have plans for the gem in Alaska, do you know where in Alaska and do you know what those plans are?"

"Hold up! Before we talk about the gem, let's address the fact that you guys just left Ronald and didn't even try to get our own teammate back! We're supposed to be a team and have each other's backs but we don't stand and fight for one another!" Susan ranted passionately.

"Susan, if we would've stayed and tried to save Ronald, it would have put us in far worse trouble. We had to get out of there to save ourselves but trust me, we will find Ronald and save him. But we have to get the gem first," Ashanti said calmly in an effort to comfort and calm Susan.

Susan knew Ashanti was right even if it still didn't feel right.

"What we need to figure out is why, out of nowhere, Ronald decided to fight us," added Robert.

"It seems to me he was under some sort of

mind control, possibly by the Gem of Faith," said Akira.

Susan looked down at her hands before adding, "That make sense considering his eyes were green and he looked lifeless."

"How do you know it was the Gem of Faith that controlled him?" Juan asked Akira.

"I don't, it's a theory. But Ronald followed Tavin when he had the gem and when he came back, he was under some type of mind control."

"How can we get him out of this mind control?" Susan wondered aloud.

"I don't even know if the gem is the real reason he's under mind control," said Akira.

Sadness washed over Susan. She had no idea if they would ever get Ronald back and that very idea concerned her.

"Are you okay, Susan?" Robert noticed the forlorn expression on Susan's face.

"I will be but we *must* make it our priority to find Ronald."

"You're right and we will," Robert said to comfort Susan.

Ashanti turned back to Akira. "Alright, let's get back to the Hostiles. Akira, you said the Hostiles are planning to do something with the gem in Alaska. Is that all you know?"

"They have a remote base on Mount McKinley and that's where they planned to transport the gem. I also saw some kind of schematic for a satellite but I'm not clear how it fits into their plan."

"Is that everything?" asked Juan.

Akira looked at him, confused. "Why would I leave something out?"

"Just an extra nudge, that's all. Everyone forgets stuff sometimes," replied Juan.

"Well, not me. I have a photographic memory."

"You have a photographic memory and you chose to be an explorer? Why not be a doctor or scientist or something like that?" Juan laughed as he asked.

"Actually I am, those are my side hobbies," Akira said, tooting her own horn.

"Hey team, let's get back to the task at hand." Robert wanted to pull the team's attention back to the mission.

"Robert's right, now that we know they have a satellite, we need to destroy it because they can't be planning anything good with it," said Ashanti.

"How can the five of us destroy a satellite?" asked Robert.

"Look around. This room is wall-to-wall with weapons. I'm sure there are some bombs around here somewhere." Ashanti stood and walked towards the back wall as she spoke.

"If not, I could always make one," Akira added with a wink.

"I take it you've never heard of humility." Juan couldn't resist commenting.

Before Akira could respond, Ashanti stepped in and got the team back on track.

"Here's what we should do. Juan, Akira, and Robert should destroy the satellite while Susan and I find the gem and Ronald."

"Are you sure we should split up? You see how well that worked out last time," Susan was more nervous this time because she knew just how badly a mission could go.

"I understand your thinking but if we're all together in a group, the Hostiles will have their attention on us and we probably won't make it anywhere near that satellite. But if we split up, they have to split up their guys too and that gives us more of a chance," said Ashanti.

"Yeah, you're right. We should also find a way to stay in constant communicate with each other. We need to update positions, situations—pretty much anything we see," said Susan.

Everyone nodded their heads in agreement.

"If we're all in agreement, let's get ready," Ashanti said.

Everyone grabbed a small, lightweight tactical

backpack and filled it with a first-aid kit, two flashbang grenades, two regular grenades, and a large flask of water. When it came to choosing their own primary weapons, the team differed in their choices. Juan's choice weapon was a large non-discreet assault rifle and a small pistol to carry on his hip holster. He also grabbed a rocket-propelled grenade, or rpg, just in case things became a bit much.

Susan grabbed two lightweight pistols and an array of daggers and knives. She also grabbed an old picture of she and Ronald on a mission, hoping that if he saw it, he would snap out of his hypnosis.

Ashanti grabbed a semi-automatic shotgun along with a small pistol. She also got her hands on some navigation equipment so she could make her way around the mountainous terrain.

Akira's weapon of choice was a small, remote-controlled fully weaponized drone. While it wasn't a light drone, Akira knew it was necessary to use against the Hostiles. The drone was a plain white in color and had a small machine gun torrent on it along with a miniature rocket. She also grabbed two pistols just in case the drone malfunctioned.

Robert packed the heaviest out of everyone. He packed specialized grenades that could go an incredible range, two small pistols, knives and daggers, and even more first-aid equipment.

With their equipment now in order, the Explorers boarded their plane. Everyone was ready except for Susan. She was scared to run into Ronald again as she feared she may never be able to get him back to the way he was before every landing on that ship. Nevertheless, she put her fears aside and prepared to grab the Gem of Faith and restore Ronald.

CHAPTER 11

ENTERING THE BATTLEFIELD

Susan, Akira, Juan, Ashanti, and Robert landed half a mile away from the Hostile's base on Mount McKinley. The whole crew wore thick white jackets and most of them were able to move comfortably except for Juan. The crew noticed how Juan couldn't move his arms in his coat but Ashanti was the only one to ask him about it.

"Juan, you okay over there? You look like the brother from *A Christmas Story*," Ashanti said as she laughed at Juan.

"I do have on a lot of layers under here."

"How many layers?" asked Ashanti.

"Two shirts, a sweater, jacket, and this coat. I think I need to strip down a little bit."

The whole team let out a few chuckles before

helping Juan remove some of his layers.

"Why would you do this to yourself?" asked Akira only half-joking.

"I live in Guam, so I'm not that used to the cold," Juan replied innocently.

After removing the sweater and jacket, Juan put on the coat and was able to move much better.

"Thanks guys," said Juan to the group.

"No problem. Besides, we're gonna need your marksman skills. You're useless without your arms," joked Robert.

A moment of levity was important for the team considering what they were about to get themselves into.

*　　*　　*　　*　　*

While the Explorers were headed towards Mount McKinley, Ronald and the other Hostiles were finishing up the satellite. When finished, the satellite would be large enough to send signals that could spread all over North America. Once the Gem of Faith is placed in the center, the gem's mind-bending powers would be able to travel through the satellite's wavelengths. If Tavin was able to complete his plan, the entire continent of North America would be under his control, giving him access to war ships, government secrets, nuclear codes, and pretty much anything he wanted. Tavin thought the world would benefit under his rule but that couldn't be farther from the truth.

Ronald and other Hostiles spent hours putting the finishing touches on the satellite. Once they felt they were finished, Ronald went down to the base to report their progress to Tavin.

"Sir, your satellite is complete," Ronald said lifelessly.

"Good, now we need to get it ready so our plan can finally be fulfilled. The world will finally know order and it'll be because of us," said Tavin.

"The world will be lucky," said Ronald.

"It sure will be. Now take a break, you deserve it."

Tavin headed towards the satellite dish with the gem in his pocket. The satellite was eleven feet tall and roughly a few hundred feet from the base. Once Tavin reached the satellite dish, his henchman stopped what they were doing and kneeled before him. Tavin made all of his henchmen think of him as a god and he relished in that belief. He then climbed up the side of the satellite dish to place the Gem of Faith in the center. The gem fit perfectly in the center. Once inside the satellite, the gem began to glow a bright green color indicating that it was working.

"In around thirty minutes, the entire continent will be under my thumb," said Tavin with a sinister grin.

* * * * *

While Ronald and the Hostiles were constructing the satellite, the Explorers were heading towards the Hostile's base preparing to take them down. As the team approached the base, they paused and went over their plan once again.

"Let's go over the details one more time. Ashanti and Susan are going to find Ronald while the rest of us destroy that big satellite over there," said Juan as he pointed to the satellite off in the distance.

"Yes, it's a simple plan. I don't know why you felt the need to go over it again," said Akira.

"I just don't want any of us to screw up the plan because the stakes are extremely high."

"Juan's right, the stakes are much higher now than before. We all need to communicate with each other and fight for each other. We're a team here and we have to have faith in each other. Now let's destroy this satellite and get our teammate back!" Ashanti said firing up the team.

This motivated the team and psyched them up for the task ahead. They got their weapons ready and walked towards the base.

CHAPTER 12

FIGHT FOR THE GEM

The Explorers walked downhill towards the Hostile's base and satellite. They moved slowly and crouched as they didn't want to draw any attention. The guards stood like mindless statues and the Explorers almost made it past them but just before they got all the way downhill, they were spotted.

"Hey!" yelled one of the guards as he saw the team passing by.

The guard pointed his gun at them but before he could pull the trigger, Susan pulled out her two pistols and shot the guard. The whole team was shocked and impressed about how quickly she reacted.

"Well, let's go," Susan said as she walked ahead of the team.

The wind disguised the sound of gunshots from Susan's pistols. After they passed the two guards, the team split up. Ashanti and Susan headed towards the base while Robert, Akira, and Juan went toward the satellite. Before they left, they all hugged each other. A sense of uncertainty moved through the group as the reality of what was happening set in. This mission could very well be the last for either of them.

"Good luck guys," Susan said as she and Ashanti went towards the base.

"Don't worry, we're not gonna need it," said Juan with confidence.

The team went their separate ways and now all they had to do was to figure out the specifics. There was a horde of Hostiles surrounding the satellite and even though they weren't very competent, they greatly outnumbered Juan, Akira, and Robert. The Explorers stood above the Hostiles on an incline in the mountain trying to figure out the best plan.

The winds howled on top of Mount McKinley and this blocked out the voices and echoes from the group's discussion.

"There are so many! How are we going to get rid of them?" asked Robert concerned they were about to fight a losing battle.

"I have a rocket on my drone. That would definitely get rid of most of them," said Akira after a few seconds.

"Don't we need that to destroy the satellite?" Robert inquired.

"No, I brought an rpg just in case something like this situation happened," said Juan.

"You prepared for this specific situation?" Akira said in a dismissing tone.

"Yes, I used foresight, unlike you," said Juan knowing it would bother Akira.

"Unlike me? I've prepared for everything," Akira said very defensively.

"If you prepared for everything, how come you didn't pack two explosives?" Juan was just messing with Akira to have fun but Akira didn't take it in a fun way and she was getting heated.

"You know what you mo—," Akira said before being interrupted.

"Guys, chill out.," Robert said, being the voice of reason.

"Right now, which one of us is going to take the satellite and who's going to get rid of the crowd?" Juan asked.

"I'll take out the satellite since my drone has enhanced accuracy features, while you'll thin out the crowd with the rpg," Akira said.

"Sounds like a plan. And by the way, I was just messing with ya earlier. You need to lighten up a bit, Akira." Juan smiled at Akira, hoping to ease any tension.

Akira paused for a second to take in what he said because she knew he was right. She did need to lighten up a bit.

Juan walked down to the incline and was close enough to the Hostiles to shoot the rpg successfully but not close enough for them to notice him.

"Alright Robert, once this rpg goes off, come down here because we'll have to fight the ones left over," Juan said through his earpiece.

"I got ya," responded Robert.

Juan pulled out the rpg he carried on his back, placed it on his shoulder and prepared to take down the horde of Hostiles surrounding the satellite.

"You guys ready?" Juan asked.

"All good," Akira said.

Juan pulled the trigger and an enormous explosion followed. The explosion took out most of the Hostiles and thinned out the crowd just like the team intended. The remaining Hostiles looked for the person responsible for the explosion but their bright green eyes made it hard for them to see.

Tavin was still around the satellite when the big explosion happened and after he saw it, he had two guards protect him. He went to the center of the satellite and grabbed the Gem of Faith. Undetected by the Explorers, Tavin was escorted back to the base by the guards.

Once the remaining Hostiles spotted Juan, they fired their weapons. Juan ducked for cover under a large rock.

"Robert, I could really use your help about now," Juan said.

Robert started rushing down to help Juan and as he was moving, two Hostiles rushed towards him. He pulled out his pistols and took out the Hostiles as he rushed down. When he reached Juan, he threw one of his specialized long-range grenades and this took out four Hostiles. He then joined Juan and took cover under the same rock as him.

"It's only a matter of time before they all get to us," said Robert.

"Yeah, that's why Akira needs to hurry up with that drone," said Juan.

"Um…I can hear you guys and I need to make

sure I get the accuracy right," came Akira's voice through the earpiece.

Akira focused on setting the target location for the rocket. Once she set the destination, she picked up the remote control and the drone went airborne. The drone went up approximately 200 feet in the air then she flipped a gray switch and pushed a red button on her controller, launching the rocket. Within a few seconds, the rocket made a direct hit on the satellite dish and blew it to pieces. Once the satellite erupted into flames, chunks of it flew all over the place and even took out a few of the Hostiles. Juan and Robert protected themselves from the debris.

After she saw the satellite blow up, Akira jumped with joy and was thrilled that her drone worked.

"Good job, Akira. Now get down here and help us get rid of these guys," said Juan.

Akira then activated the machine gun turrets on her drone and fired on a few of the Hostiles. Once the drone entered the battlefield, Juan and Robert were able to get up from their cover and fire at the guards. Ronald and Juan were taking out Hostiles, left and right and the drone was a big help to the team. After it took out a dozen of their men, the Hostiles finally shot the drone out of the sky. The drone fell to the ground, which enraged Akira.

"Oh come on!" Akira exclaimed disappointed in losing her drone. Fortunately, it lasted only a few short seconds as she ran down to help Juan and Robert.

Without the drone, the fighting got harder but they were able to pull through. With Akira's help, they were able to finish off the last of the Hostiles.

"Good job guys!" Juan said happily as they celebrated their victory with a group hug.

"Now that we have that part covered, let's go find the others," said Robert.

*　　*　　*　　*　　*

While Akira, Juan, and Robert were completing their part of the mission on the mountain, Ashanti and Susan got to the base relatively easily. Most of the attention of the guards was directed towards Robert, Akira, and Juan so Ashanti and Susan only ran into a few Hostiles.

They entered the main hallway of the base trying to be as quiet as possible. The base wasn't very large so the search for Ronald and the gem wouldn't take very long.

Suddenly, four guards entered the hallway from came a nearby room and spotted them. Susan threw a dagger at one of the guys as Ashanti returned fire on the others. Ashanti and Susan were able to quickly dispose of the Hostiles and keep moving.

"Do you think anyone else heard us?" Susan asked Ashanti.

"They probably did, so we have to be careful from now on."

Panic set in for Susan as she knew she would

have to face another Hostile horde. She also knew it was inevitable that she'd have to fight Ronald and she had no idea how she could restore him. Ashanti noticed the change in Susan's demeanor.

"Hey Susan, whatever happens, we're going to make it through. I promise."

Her words helped restore a sense of calm for Susan and they kept walking. Before Susan could thank Ashanti, eight Hostiles ran into the hallway with their guns blazing. Susan and Ashanti immediately took cover behind several large crates in the hallway. Ashanti threw a grenade that took out three of the guards. Susan shot at the guards with her pistols. With their clouded vision, the Hostiles couldn't hit Susan and Ashanti and they couldn't find cover in time. The last two Hostiles tried to retreat after their comrades had fallen but to no avail as Susan took them out.

"Let's keep moving!" yelled Ashanti.

As they neared the end of the hallway, they noticed another Hostile guard but this one looked different, he looked familiar. Ashanti raised her gun and was prepared to shoot the man but Susan pulled down Ashanti's gun.

"That's not a regular Hostile, that's Ronald." said Susan.

They knew they were going to have to fight Ronald and they prayed they would be able to restore him.

CHAPTER 13

FRIEND OR FOE

Ashanti and Susan stared at Ronald. He pulled his gun but Susan and Ashanti didn't make a move. Their goal was to try to approach him calmly, hoping it would snap him out of his mind control.

"Do you know who we are?" Susan asked him in a calm, collected voice.

"You're the enemy and you must be eliminated," replied Ronald lacking emotion.

"We're not the enemy. It's me, Susan. Ronald, I know you remember me. "

A series of images flashed in Ronald's mind of his adventures with he and Susan but he didn't really understand what was happening or what they meant.

"Do you remember when we first met, during

our mission to find *The Relic of Power*? Or remember that time we had to find the Crimson Rose and almost got killed by sumo wrestlers?"

"Sumo wrestlers?" Ashanti asked, confused.

"It's a long story, but I know Ronald has to remember that."

Faint memories reentered Ronald's mind but then he remembered the mission at hand. A look grazed his face and Susan knew he was ready to kill.

"We don't need to use our guns, we just need to subdue him and try to re-focus his mind," Susan said to Ashanti.

"What about his gun?" Ashanti asked.

"Wrestle it away from him but we don't need to kill him."

Ronald raised his pistol at Susan's head and before he could pull the trigger, Ashanti blitzed him and tried to tackle him to the ground. Ronald was able to push her away and once he did, he pointed his gun at her and started to pull the trigger. Susan threw a dagger at Ronald's hand, causing him to drop his gun. She quickly ran up behind him and put him in a chokehold. Ashanti grabbed his gun and slid it to the other end of the hallway so it was out of Ronald's reach.

"This isn't you Ronald! Try to remember who you are!" Susan pleaded with Ronald.

Ronald grabbed Susan's arm and tried to pull it from around his neck. Then he threw his head back and headbutted Susan in the nose. Susan stumbled backwards and Ashanti ran up to Ronald and gave him a forceful right hook. Ronald dodged the rest of her punches and she was able to dodge most of his. When Ronald finally landed a punch, it connected in the center of Ashanti's chest. The combined impact and pain caused her to stumble backwards and reach for her chest. Seeing her guard down, Ronald delivered a flurry of punches all over her body. Ashanti fell to her knees and without hesitation, Ronald punched her in the face with all of his might, knocking Ashanti out cold.

Ronald was ready to keep whaling on her and finish his job but before he could, he heard footsteps running down the hall. Juan, Akira, and Robert came upon them, ready to support Ashanti and Susan. When Ronald heard their footsteps, he picked up Ashanti's gun and fired in their direction. Bullets were flying everywhere and one hit Akira in the arm.

"Akira!" Robert exclaimed.

Robert pulled Akira into the nearest room off the hallway so he could patch up her arm.

After looking closely, Robert said to Akira, "You're going to be alright, it's just a flesh wound. We just need to apply pressure and you'll be fine."

Robert pulled out his first-aid kit, grabbed a towel, and applied pressure to Akira's wound. Ashanti collapsed into the room still holding her chest.

Back in the hallway, the battle was still being waged.

Click! Click!

It was the sound of Ronald's empty clip. Juan raised his gun and aimed it at Ronald, ready to shoot him in the leg.

Click!

Juan was also out of ammo.

"Of all the times to run out of ammo, it had to be now." Juan mumbled to himself.

Ronald and Juan looked at one another and ran towards the other. Juan landed the first punch which went right to Ronald's jaw. He then hit Ronald in the chest and went to follow up with another but Ronald caught his fist in mid-air. Once he caught Juan's punch, Ronald kneed him in the stomach and hit him in the throat. Ronald started to do the same thing to Juan as he did to Ashanti but Susan saw this and knew she had to help Juan.

Susan's head was still throbbing from earlier but she was able to power through the pain. She tackled Ronald from behind and pulled him to the ground. Once on the ground, Susan grabbed one of her daggers and stabbed Ronald in the shoulder.

She knew this would immobilize him but it wouldn't be fatal. Afterwards, she went over to check on Juan.

"Are you okay?" Susan asked holding out her hand to help him up.

"Yeah, did you kill him?"

"No, I just immobilized him. There has to be a way to get him back though."

Footsteps approached from around the corner. Susan and Juan turned around and drew their weapons. Tavin appeared holding the Gem of Faith in one hand and a loaded pistol in the other.

"You take another step and it'll be the last one you take," Juan said to Tavin.

Juan and Susan both had their weapons pointed at Tavin and they had a clear advantage against him. Juan was ready to pull the trigger and end Tavin but before he could, a grenade rolled behind him. He kicked the grenade in the air avoiding the explosion, then three Hostiles ran into the hallway. They came in, guns blazing, and forced Juan and Susan to take cover. Juan ran into the room where Robert was patching up Akira. Susan ran in that same direction but was grabbed by Tavin before she could make it through the door. She wanted to break free but he was holding her at gunpoint.

The four Explorers were shoulder-to-shoulder in the small, brightly-lit storage room. Fortunately, there were plenty of boxes and items to use for cover.

"You had to bring them in here?" Robert said to Juan wondering why he'd lead the Hostiles in their direction.

Tavin was distracted by the sounds coming from down the hall and Susan was able to break free with a powerful headbutt. Tavin fell backwards but still had his gun pointed at Susan and the gem in the opposite hand.

"Just because you destroyed my satellite doesn't mean my mission is over. I will bring order to the world even if I have to control people one at a time!" yelled Tavin.

"The world doesn't need you to bring order," Susan said.

"If I don't, who will? The Gem of Faith is a powerful artifact and deserves to be used to its full potential."

"You're delusional."

"Maybe I am, but I was able to control your partner and use him as my little puppet."

"You need to stop," Susan said enraged.

"If Ronald was the one that trained you, that means you would be a useful asset to me as well."

Tavin raised the Gem of Faith from his left hand and pointed it at Susan's head. It cast a beam that went directly to Susan's head. If he could control Ronald's prodigy, he could use them both to help destroy the Explorers. Tavin was ecstatic about his plan working until he noticed that Susan had no reaction to the gem's power. Susan didn't feel any of the same pain that Ronald did. In fact, she felt nothing from the energy beam.

Susan walked over and grabbed Tavin's hand, stopping the energy beam. Susan then punched Tavin in his face, making him fall to the ground. Susan's belief in herself and her team was strong enough to where the Gem of Faith's mind-bending powers weren't strong enough to alter her mind. Susan grabbed his gun from his right hand and grabbed the Gem of Faith from his left. She held the gun to his head and demanded to know how to restore Ronald.

"How do I fix Ronald?"

Tavin was so scared for his life, he actually told her the truth.

"In order to fix him, you have to use the Gem of Faith on him," Tavin said, shaking and scared.

Susan looked at Tavin and contemplated whether to kill him or not. As long as Tavin lived, he would hunt the gem. That made he him too dangerous to be left alive. Susan made a hard decision as she didn't want to kill anybody but she knew Tavin had to go. It was a difficult choice but one she had to make. She pulled the trigger and saw the life quickly drain from Tavin's body. She then walked over to Ronald who was still on the ground from his stab wound. He'd left the dagger in so he wouldn't bleed out but he was still in immense pain. He stood as Susan walked towards him. He was prepared to fight. Susan pointed the Gem of Faith at his head hoping Tavin was telling the truth. A green beam of energy emitted from the gem and casted onto Ronald's forehead. Ronald didn't feel pain this time but instead, he felt a sense of relief. He could see all types of memories from his life coming back into his head and he started to feel control of his own mind. After almost one minute, Ronald passed out. Susan rushed over to him thinking she had killed him.

"Ronald! Ronald! Come on, wake up!" Susan exclaimed.

Ronald woke back up and instead of his eyes being a bright green, they were back to their normal brown. He looked around and saw Susan standing over him.

"Susan!" Ronald said with a mix of confusion and joy.

Susan hugged him as she was just happy to have her old friend back.

"What happened to me and why is there a knife in my back?" Ronald asked.

"Sorry, but you were evil for a little bit so I might have stabbed you in the back," said Susan.

Juan, Robert, and Akira all walked out of the room.

"Is he the good Ronald or the one you had to stab?" Juan quipped.

"It's me. I'm back to normal now," said Ronald.

"Great, I didn't want to have to shoot you," said Juan.

They all went over to greet Ronald and celebrate his return. The team had succeeded in their mission. Ronald was restored and they were able to secure the Gem of Faith.

CHAPTER 14

A NEW LIFE

With the Gem of Faith in hand, the Explorers went all around the base, restoring the remaining 108 Hostiles.

Once they finished, they boarded their plane and headed back to Melody's house in New York to deliver the gem.

"Tell me, did anything exciting happen on the mission?" Melody asked the team.

"It's a long story," Ronald replied.

"Uh-oh, I don't want to hear it. The main thing is you all delivered the gem and you're alive. Good work. From the looks of it, you make a great team," said Melody.

"Yes, I think we do," said Susan.

Melody placed the gem in a discreet and secure location known only by she and her superiors. She also transferred *The Relic of Power* to this facility as she felt they were equally dangerous.

After they delivered the gem and completed the mission, the Explorers headed back to their home countries. Even though they were going to their respective homes, they still needed to stay connected just in case they had to find another artifact. Especially one with the power of the Gem of Faith.

Everyone was excited to return home and get back to exploring except for Ronald. After being controlled and nearly killing all of his teammates, he wanted to take a break from exploring. He decided to tell Susan about his decision. He waited until they walked into Martin's old office at the Museum of Important Artifacts.

"Susan, I've been doing a lot of thinking about everything and after what happened on this mission, I need to take a break from exploring."

The statement shocked Susan but she understood how he came to that conclusion.

"Are you sure? This is such a big decision, Ronald. You love exploring. Are you sure you want to give it up?"

"I'm not giving it up, I just need some time to recover and explore other aspects of my life."

"I understand, now I just wonder who's going to be my new partner."

"Susan, from what you've shown me from this last mission, you don't need a partner anymore. You're no longer the amateur I had to train and coach. You've become your own explorer now and I'm proud of you."

"Thank you, Ronald."

His words meant a lot to Susan and it boosted her confidence. They shared a hug before Ronald headed home. Susan stayed in the museum and went to the artifact collection room. She looked at all the artifacts Ronald had collected alone as well as those with her. She knew she would have to live up to Ronald's legacy as an explorer. Instead of being intimidated, she felt happy that she had an opportunity to become a great explorer like Ronald along with an extraordinary team to back her up.

Susan and the rest of the Explorers slept easy knowing the Gem of Faith was secure and out of danger.